This igloo book belongs to:

....

Published in 2020
First published in the UK by Igloo Books Ltd
An imprint of Igloo Books Ltd
Cottage Farm, NN6 0BJ, UK
Owned by Bonnier Books
Sveavägen 56, Stockholm, Sweden
www.igloobooks.com

1120 007
10 12 14 15 13 11
ISBN 978-1-78197-629-6

Illustrated by Marcin Piwowarski
Written by Adrian Rees

Printed and manufactured in China

Cheeky Little Kittens

igloobooks

It was very early in the morning and the
sun was just beginning to rise.
Gus and Gally, two little kittens, were curled up
together on a cushion, fast asleep.

Suddenly, two little eyes **popped** open.

Gus **stretched** his little legs and sat up.

Gally raised his head and **yawned**.

The kittens wanted to play. They didn't know it, but they were about to have a **very** exciting time, indeed.

Today was the day that Gus and Gally were going outside for the very first time.

They rubbed the
sleep from their eyes
with their paws and
ran
all
the
way
downstairs.

The kittens were very hungry after their long sleep and *rushed* to the kitchen. They **gulped** down their food very quickly and then had a drink of water.

Instead of going back upstairs to play, they heard
Jenny, the little girl that they lived with, open the
kitchen door and call to them.

"Come on, you two," said Jenny. "Today we are going on a **big** adventure outside!"

Jenny walked through the door and Gus and Gally ran after her and then **skidded** to a halt.

The kittens couldn't believe their **eyes** or their **ears** or their **noses**. What wonderful **sights** and **sounds** and **smells**!
Gus jumped down the step and ran along the path.

Gally was a bit frightened.
He stayed on the doorstep,
peering out.

"Come on, Gally," said Jenny. "Don't be shy," and she
scooped him up and carried him onto the grass.

Gus was already rolling over and over on the lawn.
He **loved** the way it tickled his back.
Gally watched him, but **clung** to Jenny.
This was much too scary for him.

Suddenly, a plane
flew overhead,
making lots of noise.

Vrooom !

Gally jumped out of Jenny's arms and
hid under a bush.

Gus ran after him and the kittens peered out,
their eyes as **big** as saucers.

Jenny laughed. "It's only a plane," she said. Slowly, the two little kittens c r e p t back onto the lawn.

A butterfly fluttered past and Gus chased it, but it flew too high for him to catch it.

The wind blew a leaf across the grass.

Gally crouched down and then jumped after the leaf and caught it. Clever Gally!

Gus spotted something moving in the flower bed. What could it be?

He rushed up and a **huge** bird with flapping wings **burst** out from behind the flowers. Gus meowed loudly.

"It's only a bird," said Jenny. "It won't hurt you!"
Gally clung to Jenny's leg.
He didn't like the bird at all.

The two kittens had just stopped shaking when Jenny's father appeared, mowing the lawn with a very **noisy** mower! Gally was so frightened, he **shot** inside Jenny's jacket and Gus **leapt** on top of her head!

It took Jenny quite a while to calm them both down.
In fact, she had to give them one or two of their special
treats before they stopped shaking.

Jenny carried the kittens around the garden, showing them the lovely flowers.

Buzzzz!

Gally jumped down to sniff one, but leapt back quickly when an **angry** bee flew out at him.

"It's only a bee, silly," said Jenny.
"It won't hurt you."

**Woof!
Woof!**

Seconds later, a **huge**, hairy dog
popped his shaggy head over the
fence and barked loudly. The kittens
shot off down the garden.

Gus and Gally stopped behind a bush and caught
their breath. Then, they heard a **whooshing** sound.
Suddenly, Jenny's little brother, Kevin, appeared and
soaked them with the garden hose.
He thought it was very funny.

Jenny was very angry. "Kevin!" she yelled.
"Stop scaring the kittens!"

Kevin just laughed louder and rolled on the grass.
Gus and Gally didn't hear. They were too busy
rushing into the house.

Gus and Gally were once again curled up together on their cushions. They were very tired. Outside was far too exciting for two little kittens. Maybe they would try again tomorrow.